This book belongs to:

....

....

Quarto is the authority on a wide range of topics.

Quarto educates, entertains and enriches the lives of our readers—enthusiasts and lovers of hands-on living. www.quartoknows.com

Author and illustrator: Anna Shuttlewood
Editor: Harriet Stone
Designer: Victoria Kimonidou

© 2018 Quarto Publishing plc

This edition first published in 2018 by QED Publishing,
an imprint of The Quarto Group.
The Old Brewery, 6 Blundell Street,
London N7 9BH, United Kingdom.
T (0)20 7700 6700 F (0)20 7700 8066
www.QuartoKnows.com

All rights reserved. No part of this publication may be reproduced, stored in a retrieval system, or transmitted in any form or by any means, electronic, mechanical, photocopying, recording, or otherwise, without the prior permission of the publisher, nor be otherwise circulated in any form of binding or cover other than that in which it is published and without a similar condition being imposed on the subsequent purchaser.

A catalogue record for this book is available from the British Library.

ISBN 978 1 91241 383 6

Manufactured in Guangdong, China CC072018

9 8 7 6 5 4 3 2 1

FSC
www.fsc.org
MIX
Paper from
responsible sources
FSC® C008047

The Prettiest Flower

by Anna Shuttlewood

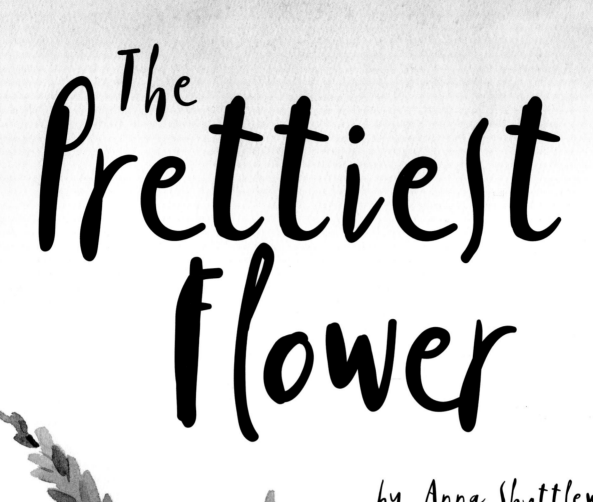

Hedgehog had a beautiful garden.
She carefully looked after it every day.

It was so pretty and tidy that people often stopped to admire it, or to ask for cuttings from her beautiful plants.

Hedgehog liked colourful flowers best - her favourites were sunflowers. They grow so tall!

She also grew red snapdragons,

a variety of
geraniums,

blue lupines,

pink and
white cosmos

and scented
lavender.

In the corner there was a clump of
forget-me-nots. Hedgehog didn't plant
them, but she cared for them anyway.
Blue was her favourite colour.

But, one morning, Hedgehog looked out in horror at her garden. It had been ruined! Most of her plants were broken or squashed and all their leaves had been chewed!

Hedgehog was very upset.
She worked hard all day tidying
and replanting her garden.
Finally, she was finished.

But the next morning, Hedgehog
found that her beautiful garden
had been destroyed again!

It must be my neighbour,
Hare, thought Hedgehog.

"Do you think it's okay to eat other people's plants?" Hedgehog asked Hare, upset. "Can't you grow your own, in your own garden? I work all day to make mine beautiful, while others laze about!"

"It wasn't me! I have far better things to be doing than eating your flowers!" replied Hare, pointing to a pile of books by his chair.

If it wasn't Hare, then who could it be?
Hedgehog had another idea.

"Mrs. Duck, I would
like a word with you,"
said Hedgehog. "Your
children have been in my
garden during the night and
have eaten all my flowers!"

"My ducklings? They certainly have not been in your garden! They are at school all morning and are asleep with me all night."

If it's not the ducklings, then it must be Mole, Hedgehog thought.

"Mole, I am so disappointed in you! I never thought you would be so mean!" said Hedgehog.

"You are mistaken," said Mole. "I did not eat your flowers; I only eat yummy insects."

If it wasn't Mole, then who could it be? Hedgehog was determined to find out.

Hedgehog went sadly back to her garden to fix it again. But this time she had a cunning plan.

When night time came Hedgehog was ready. She waited silently in her garden. It wasn't long before she noticed some movement among the geraniums.

"Caught you, thief!" cried Hedgehog,
jumping down from her ladder.

It was Caterpillar!

Caterpillar was so startled that he started to cry.
Hedgehog felt sorry for the little animal. She agreed
that if Caterpillar stopped eating her plants, she
would leave out a plate of lettuce for him each day.

Caterpillar kept Hedgehog company while
she worked in her garden. They shared
many happy days together, enjoying:

cups of tea,

lots of strawberries,

fairy tales,

afternoon naps

and late nights
watching the stars.

One day, Caterpillar
didn't come for his lettuce.

It wilted, uneaten, in the sun.

I wonder where Caterpillar's gone,
thought Hedgehog, sadly.

She tended her garden, looking after her beautiful flowers,

had cups of tea and strawberries

and stayed up late to watch the stars.

But it just wasn't the same without Caterpillar.

Then, one morning, Hedgehog found
a beautiful new flower in her garden.

"Caterpillar, you've turned into
a butterfly!" Hedgehog cried.
"I'm so pleased you've returned!
You are certainly the prettiest
flower that has ever grown
in my garden."

Next Steps

Discussion and Comprehension

Discuss the story with the children and ask the following questions, encouraging them to take turns and give full answers if they are able to. Offer support by turning to the appropriate pages of the book for support if needed.

- What did you like most about this story?
- Which flowers did Hedgehog like to grow in her garden? Have you heard of any of these flowers before?
- What colour are the flowers? How many different colours can you see in the garden?
- Can you remember who Hedgehog thought had ruined the garden?
- What was Hedgehog's cunning plan?
- What happened to Caterpillar? Do you know what is hanging in the tree on page 20?

Descriptive Sentences

Ask the children to decide which they think is the prettiest flower and why. Make a list of words together that describe the flowers e.g. how they look, how they might feel, how they might smell. Explain that these describing words are called adjectives. Give the children each a piece of paper with a floral border. Ask them to choose flowers from the book and write sentences that describe them. Show an example first: *The sunflowers have long green stems and bright yellow petals. Lavender has small purple and blue petals.* If they are able, encourage children to underline the adjectives. Give the children time to illustrate their sentences.

Life Cycle on a Paper Plate

Give each child a paper plate that you have divided into four sections and labelled Eggs, Caterpillar, Chrysalis and Butterfly. Show the children a finished plate with: a green leaf and three small dried white beans for the eggs; a piece of fusilli pasta for the caterpillar; a pasta shell for the chrysalis and a piece of bow tie pasta for the butterfly. Ask the children to create their own lifecycle using glue to stick the pasta, beans and leaf in the correct sections. They can use paint to colour the chrysalis, caterpillar and butterfly stages.